MW00756713

Maple

Maple

Lori Nichols

SCHOLASTIC INC.

For Harper, Zoe and Bella

No part of this publication may be reproduced, stored in a retrieval system, or transmitted in any form
or by any means, electronic, mechanical, photocopying, recording, or otherwise,
without written permission of the publisher. For information regarding permission, write to
Nancy Paulsen Books, a division of Penguin Young Readers Group, a member of Penguin Group (USA) LLC,
A Penguin Random House Company, 345 Hudson Street, New York, NY 10014.

ISBN 978-0-545-85899-1

Copyright © 2014 by Lori Nichols. All rights reserved.
Published by Scholastic Inc., 557 Broadway, New York, NY 10012,
by arrangement with Nancy Paulsen Books, a division of Penguin Young Readers Group,
a member of Penguin Group (USA) LLC, A Penguin Random House Company.
SCHOLASTIC and associated logos are trademarks and/or registered trademarks of Scholastic Inc.

12 11 10 9 8 7 6 5 4 3 2 1   15 16 17 18 19 20/0

Printed in the U.S.A.   40

First Scholastic printing, March 2015

Design by Marikka Tamura
Text set in LTC Kennerley Pro
The illustrations for this book were rendered in pencil on Mylar and then digitally colored.

Maple loved her name.

When she was still a whisper,
her parents planted a tiny tree in her honor!

And even though
Flavia,
Millie Jane,
Lena,
Lily,
and Constance
were all good names . . .

Maple was the perfect fit.

And as Maple grew . . .

so did her tree.

Sometimes, when Maple was noisy
(which was a lot),
her parents sent her outside to play.
Her tree didn't mind if she was loud.

Maple would sing to her tree . . .

and sway for her tree . . .

and sometimes even pretend to be a tree!

On some days, when the wind was just right,
Maple would simply lie under her tree,
and its leaves would dance just for her.

Then one day, Maple noticed her tree was bare.
Maple was worried her tree might get cold.

So Maple took off her jacket . . .

and gave it to the tree to stay warm.

Sometimes Maple wished she had someone else to play with.
(The tree wasn't very good at throwing snowballs.)

She wondered if the tree felt the same way.

So Maple introduced her tree
to a friend.

That friendship didn't last.

But Maple and her tree still had each other.

Through winter . . . and spring!

Then one day, something
surprising happened.

Then something
really surprising happened.

Maple became a big sister.

Maple tried to be a good big sister.

If the baby was cold,
Maple gave the baby her hat and gloves.

If the baby was lonely,
Maple would share her special friends.

But Maple couldn't always
make the baby happy.

And when the baby was noisy
(which was a lot),
Maple would take her outside to play.

And something magical happened.

Maple's tree danced for them both . . .

and there was just enough room under the tree
for Maple and her little sister . . . Willow.